The Horse by the Tree

by Kimberly Lecar

Illustrated by Danny Caro

Eli Books

Continue to smile & rejoice! You are loved!
Kimberly Lecar

Early in the mornings
The sun rises in the east.

While Abba starts his day
tending to the flock
Willow waits down by the tree.

Mr. Flight chirps his morning song.

Flies down to greet him

To see what's wrong.

Why are you so sad?
There are many things in which you can be glad.

Tis' another day
for you to play!

My Abba is gone,

and I feel my heart,

can no longer sing a song.

Take heart, my friend!
Tis' only for a moment.

Abba will be back before you know it.

Each day that goes by,
I ask myself why?
Why, do I get tied to this tree?

I look at this tree,

dancing with the summer breeze.

It bends and sways,

yet it's always okay.

But what you don't see are the roots beneath.

Its leaves sing songs as the wind whispers by.

With its roots digging deep as it reaches for the sky.

So, smile, <u>rejoice!</u>

Lift up your voice!

You will always be

Abba's first choice.

Mr. Flight, you are right!
I can S·I·N·G and dance.
I can stand tall and strong.
I can sway like the trees.

Because my Abba will always love me.